Sara Watson works in the HR department for a large investment firm and for years has had dreams about a guy with emerald green eyes in a place under water with a pink sky. Although in her waking life she is terrified of water, they make wild passionate love in her dreams in the Golden City under the sea. She thinks she's crazy, even more so when he, Thane, walks into her office. Thane convinces her to come with him under the sea, even though she is terrified. But when Thane is injured and loses his memory, Sara is all alone in a strange world where she's considered an outsider. Can Sara convince Thane she is his chosen mate, or will she be sent back to own world, doomed to a loveless, unhappy life?

KUDOS for *Under the Pink Sky*

In *Under the Pink Sky* by Tara Eldana, Sara Watson is shocked and dismayed when the man she has been dreaming about for ages shows up at her work and asks her to come with him under the sea, especially since Sara is terrified of water. She reluctantly agrees but then her dream lover, Thane, is injured and loses his memory. Now Sara is all alone, still terrified, and unwelcome in Thane's world. Should she go back home to her lonely, unhappy life, or hope that Thane will come to his senses before it's too late? Like the rest of her books in the Merepeople series, this one is fun, sexy, and a worthy addition to the series. ~ *Taylor Jones, The Review Team of Taylor Jones & Regan Murphy*

Under the Pink Sky by Tara Eldana is the fifth book in her mermaid series. In this story, Sara Watson is an HR manager for a large investment firm. For years she has been having very realistic dreams involving Thane, a man who lives under the sea. Sara is terrified of the water, but that doesn't seem to matter in her dreams. Thane lives in a crystal city under the sea—where the sky is pink, not blue—and Sara visits him there every night in her dreams. By day, she is lonely and unhappy and worries that she may be going insane because her dreams are so real. Then one day, Thane shows up at her work. He convinces Sara to leave everything she knows and come with him under the sea. Thane's mother hates her and wants Thane to mate with one of his own kind, not a human. But Thane is determined to have Sara...until he is injured and loses his memory. Now, Sara is alone and unwelcome in a world very different from her own. *Under the Pink Sky* is charming, clever, and intriguing. The sex scenes are hot and spicy and the action fast paced. Another jewel in the crown of this talented author. ~ *Regan Murphy, The Review Team of Taylor Jones & Regan Murphy*

Other Books by

Tara Eldana

and

Black Opal Books

Reclaiming Lexi
Double Dare
Cabin Fever

The Merpeople Series

Under the Riptides
In the Depths
On Thin Ice
Restoring Ainsley

ACKNOWLEDGMENTS

For the support and kick in the pants from the rocking members of the Greater Detroit Romance Writers of America.

To the staff and writers at Black Opal Books.

To my husband and family for everything.

Under the
PINK SKY

Tara Eldana

A Black Opal Books Publication

GENRE: STEAMY ROMANCE/PARANORMAL ROMANCE

This is a work of fiction. Names, places, characters and incidents are either the product of the author's imagination or are used fictitiously, and any resemblance to any actual persons, living or dead, businesses, organizations, events or locales is entirely coincidental. All trademarks, service marks, registered trademarks, and registered service marks are the property of their respective owners and are used herein for identification purposes only. The publisher does not have any control over or assume any responsibility for author or third-party websites or their contents.

UNDER THE PINK SKY
Copyright © 2019 by Tara Eldana
Cover Design by Jackson Cover Designs
All cover art copyright © 2019
All Rights Reserved
Print ISBN: 9781644371633

First Publication: JULY 2019

All rights reserved under the International and Pan-American Copyright Conventions. No part of this book may be reproduced or transmitted in any form or by any means, electronic or mechanical, including photocopying, recording, or by any information storage and retrieval system, without permission in writing from the publisher.

WARNING: The unauthorized reproduction or distribution of this copyrighted work is illegal. Criminal copyright infringement, including infringement without monetary gain, is investigated by the FBI and is punishable by up to 5 years in federal prison and a fine of $250,000. Anyone pirating our ebooks will be prosecuted to the fullest extent of the law and may be liable for each individual download resulting therefrom.

ABOUT THE PRINT VERSION: If you purchased a print version of this book without a cover, you should be aware that the book is stolen property. It was reported as "unsold and destroyed" to the publisher, and neither the author nor the publisher has received any payment for this "stripped book."

IF YOU FIND AN EBOOK OR PRINT VERSION OF THIS BOOK BEING SOLD OR SHARED ILLEGALLY, PLEASE REPORT IT TO: lpn@blackopalbooks.com

Published by Black Opal Books **http://www.BLACKOPALBOOKS.com**

DEDICATION

For everyone who has looked at the shimmering ocean or a lake and wondered…what if.

Chapter 1

Sara had well and truly lost it.

There was no other explanation.

Who else had a different life every time they went to sleep? In college, she had discussed it with a therapist who basically thought she was strung out on drugs.

But she never took anything, not even an aspirin. And she nursed one light beer or the same glass of wine all night long.

Each night, she was always bound to *him* in some way in a place very different from her waking life. By day, she worked in the HR department of a large investment firm, a job which she'd been lucky to land after she finished her degree.

In her dreams, the sky was pink, not blue, and she was naked or wearing a flowing white gown of gossamer fabric and walking barefoot. Water was everywhere—trickling along marble floors, reflecting rainbows rushing down jagged crystals, spraying mist scented with ambergris, and shimmering in deep pools for healing.

And the thing was—she hated the water.

She lived in Michigan, and she was surrounded by it. She had a water-skiing mishap as a kid and she was towed underwater for several feet, too terrified to let go of the tow. She nearly drowned.

He, the man in her dreams, had eyes the same shade of green as the healing pools in her nocturnal home. His sandy brown hair fell to his shoulders. He had a toned surfer's body with golden skin and a hairless chest like the other males.

She'd never seen him in her waking life.

Until now.

Panic swamped her, and she had to force herself to breathe.

He stood with Doug, her creep of a boss, and a group of people she'd never seen in the office before. He stood taller than all of them, well over six feet. He stared at her and pulled absently on the collar of the white shirt he wore without a tie, business casual style. A faint smile played along his full, sensual lips.

My God, she thought, I know how he tastes.

She wrenched her eyes away from him and dropped her shaking hands to her lap. Cold sweat trickled down her back. He broke away from the group and strode up to her desk.

"Sara," he said her name with the deep, melodic tone she knew so well from her dreams.

"How do you know my name?" The words flew out of Sara's mouth before she could stop them. Doug looked pissed and pointedly stared at her name placard that hung on the wall behind her.

"Did you need something, Thane?" Doug asked.

"No, not from you," Thane said, his eyes never leaving her face. He spoke with an accent different from the Midwestern tones she grew up with.

"You're from New Zealand, right?" she blurted out.

Doug glared.

"There and other places," Thane said.

"You all should see our IT division for our North American operations," Doug said.

He made no move to leave her desk. "I'll catch up," he said.

Doug stalked off. She sighed. There would be hell to pay. He was pissed at her for speaking out of turn, or speaking at all, and would likely dump especially tedious, boring work on her. Doug held firm to the belief that new employees should be seen and not heard, especially by clients or company bigwigs.

She figured Thane had to be a client, rather than a

company guy, with his longish hair and casual clothes.

He smiled. "Show me the break room,"

Her mouth went dry. He touched her arm briefly as she stepped past him. Electricity singed her nerve endings. She fought the crazy urge to turn into his arms and press her cheek against strong, corded neck.

She winced at her old skirt and blouse. Several eyes followed them as they made their way to the break room. They had to be wondering what a peon like her was doing with him. She knew she looked okay when she put some effort into bringing out her blue eyes and doing something with her auburn hair, which she'd scraped back into a ponytail today.

She worked out a few times a week and her figure wasn't too bad when she didn't wear shapeless, baggy clothes like she'd worn today.

"Here it is." She turned to leave.

He touched her arm again.

"Stay," he said.

He guided her to a chair and helped himself to two cups of coffee. He set a cup in front of her and she took a tentative sip with shaky hands. It was the way she liked it—two creams and no sugar.

"How did you?" She stared at him and then clamped her lips shut. She had to stop talking or she would tell him she dreamed of him every night and he and everyone she worked with would know she was a nut case.

She decided to change the subject. "How long are you here for?"

Her hand rested on her coffee cup. He reached over and brushed his thumb against her wrist where her pulse raced.

"As long as we want," he said.

He smelled like the ambergris in her dreams.

She shook her head to clear it. She had to stay in reality. "You must have plans with your colleagues," she said.

She gulped the hot coffee, burning her throat.

He took firm hold of her wrist. "With you, Sara."

"Ahem." Doug stood in the doorway to the break room. He frowned. "Sara,"

"Right," she said.

She stood up, knocking her coffee over, soaking her skirt. Thane was beside her instantly.

"Are you hurt? Did this burn your skin?" he said.

"N—no." She held the soiled material away from her thigh, glad the skirt was so baggy.

"Clean up then, come on," Doug said. "I need to line you up."

Thane bristled.

She smiled at him at him and shrugged. Real life sucked. When she made to move past him, he stood and put his hand on her shoulder. Her eyes flew to his, the most vivid green she'd ever seen, like emeralds—her mother's birthstone. Her father had given her all her mother's jewelry when she died two years before of pancreatic cancer.

"No," Thane said. "I want her with me."

Her shoulders tingled at his gentle touch.

Thane smiled at her. "I have staff issues I want her take on."

Doug looked aghast. "There are more experienced people," he said. His smirk was cruel. "I would be happy to advise you."

Thane squeezed her shoulder and waved his other hand dismissively at Doug. "I want a fresh take on this. She stays with me," he said.

Doug stomped off.

"Get your things," Thane said.

She felt waves of panic surge through her chest and gasped for breath. "I can't," she said.

He stepped closer to her. "Can't what, Sara?"

She shivered at the way he said her name, musically almost. "Doug's my boss. I need this job. I just signed a lease on my place. I can't piss him off." Her words came out in a rush.

"He's a jerk," Thane said. "He doesn't deserve you."

She looked down at her shapeless skirt and baggy blouse, which she'd picked up at a thrift store. "You're sweet, but I'm lowest grade staff member here, nobody really."

He said something in a language she didn't understand then took hold of her waist.

She gasped at the relief she felt and embarrassed by the wetness that flooded her core. She had done things with guys, but she was still technically a virgin, mostly because what she felt with the few guys she'd tried to be with didn't compare with her dreams. And the man of her dreams had his hands on her waist.

He stared at her with those amazing green eyes. "Don't ever say that again, Sara."

She went boneless at the sound of her name on his lips. "S—say what?" she said.

He pulled her against his muscled chest. "That you're nobody," he whispered before he set her away from him. "Get your stuff."

People gawked at them as they walked back to HR. Becky, her friend in IT, mouthed "WTF?" when she caught her eye.

Sara picked up her battered purse and the shopping bag with her peanut butter sandwich and grapes. "Where are we going?" She forced her voice to stay steady. "Did you reserve a conference room? They're strict about that."

"No, we're leaving," he said.

Holy hell. His New Zealand accent was doing things to her. He put his hand on the small of her back and walked her toward the elevator.

"Are you sure this is okay?" she said as she stepped into the elevator and he pushed the down button. "Where are we going?"

"The water," he said.

She jerked away from him, panic swelling her throat. "I can't. I don't swim. I don't do water or boats."

He pushed a button and stopped the elevator between floors. He lifted her chin and she swallowed hard. "Breathe, Sara." He pressed her hand against his hard, muscled chest. "Breathe, with me, now," he commanded, lifting her chin with his other hand.

She had been staring at the floor. Now she stared at his face and felt his heart thunder. She did as he commanded until her panic dissolved. He kept hold of her hand and chin.

"I will keep you safe, always, Sara."

Her toes curled at the way he almost sang her name.

"Do you trust me?" he said.

Did she? Did she trust her own crazy brain or her equally crazy dreams?

"Your choice," he murmured a word he'd whispered to her in her dreams.

Her eyes went wide.

"You can choose to stay here and work for that jerk or you are free to leave." His hands moved to her waist. "With me, Sara."

Was she free? Her father had remarried barely a year after her mother died. Irene, his new wife, was kind to her, but she had three daughters of her own. Sara's college friends, Greta and Livvy, had found jobs on the west coast, and Sara had been her parents' only child. Irene's daughters were pleasant but Sara felt like an outsider. She shut her eyes.

He deserved to know what a hot mess she was before this went any further.

"I dreamed you," she said.

"Open your eyes."

She shook her head. "I can't. I dream of you in a place with a pink sky and water everywhere and we—"

"Sara."

His voice held a bite of command and she opened her eyes, afraid of how he would look at her, but he looked at her so tenderly she went weak in her knees and would have sunk to the ground if he hadn't been holding her.

"We are together in our dreams," he said.

Our? He said our.

She nodded. He murmured a strange word and touched his lips to hers. He teased her lips open with his tongue, and she caught his tongue between her teeth. He moaned. She could feel his erection.

He stepped back, breathing hard. "You must choose, Sara."

She wasn't right in her head. She couldn't be. But she wanted him, big time. "All right," she said.

He shut his eyes and expelled a breath. "Say my name," he said He laced his fingers through hers then lifted her chin. "Say I choose you, Thane."

"I choose you, Thane."

He pulled her into his arms and claimed her mouth again. She raked her fingers through his hair. He pushed her skirt up and backed her against the wall. She was lost to everything except him. He tweaked her nipples into aching points. His tongue plunged into her mouth. Her panties were soaked with her arousal. He slipped his hand over her smooth mound she'd inexplicably shaved that morning then pressed down on her throbbing clit. She came apart, saw stars, and screamed his name.

Then everything went black.

Chapter 2

Sara opened her eyes and stared at a pink sky.

She was naked, alone, and spread out on white cushions in a room filled with crystals. She wore a necklace of deep green stones around her neck that dipped to the cleavage between her breasts. The stones glittered in the light reflected from the crystals.

Two women entered. Both wore their hair in elaborate up-dos and glided across the room in purple gauzy gowns. They gestured toward her, saying words in a language she couldn't understand. Both women appeared to be older than Sara although their faces were unlined. One woman looked at her with kind turquoise eyes, but hatred blazed from the other woman who had green eyes the same shade as Thane's.

Sara resisted the urge to scream for Thane. She wanted to hold her own with this woman. She thought of her mother Cinda's strength in fighting her cancer and grace in the face of death. Sara steeled her spine, sat up, resisted the urge to cover herself, and smiled at the women.

"Do you speak English?" she said, keeping her smile firmly in place.

The woman with the kind blue eyes smiled. "A bit," she said. She spoke with a New Zealand accent.

The green-eyed woman looked at Sara with disdain. The blue-eyed woman spoke sharply to her, and she shrugged then left them.

The blue-eyed woman patted Sara's arm. "Thane's mother Bruna. She is my sister." She looked to where the other woman had walked from the chamber. "I'm Calista." She fingered Sara's necklace, seemingly not bothered by Sara's nudity, and smiled. "Thane has claimed you."

"Claimed me?"

"Yes." Calista led Sara down a hallway to a room filled with gauzy gowns in shades of sea foam, turquoise, and dazzling white.

"I'm dreaming again," she said as Thane's aunt helped her into a white, fitted gown with a low neckline.

Calista arranged the emerald necklace so it lay against the neckline. She motioned for Sara to sit down, pulled out a comb, and worked it through her hair. Nobody except her mother had ever combed her hair and tears welled in her eyes.

Calista dropped the comb. "I hurt you," she said.

Sara squeezed Calista's hand. Her skin was soft as a baby's. "No, my mother did this. She's gone now."

Calista made soothing noises and picked up the comb. "Your hair is beautiful," she said.

Sara looked doubtfully at her boring brown hair, pointed to Calista's blonde hair, and made circular motions with her hands. "You rock that hairstyle." She lightly touched a jewel nestled in Calista's hair.

Calista grinned. "I rock."

Sara giggled. Calista combed through her hair then braided it so it hung over her shoulder. She stuck tiny floral blossoms that looked like lilacs in the thick braid then rubbed oil that smelled like lavender on her face, neck, and arms.

"You rock," Calista said.

Sara laughed. Calista led her out of the room. Sara walked barefoot on what felt like marble. Calista also walked barefoot. They entered a great hall that looked like a cavern with a pink sky. White crystal tipped with gold jutted out from the cavern walls like trickles of water that had frozen.

Her dreams had never been so real. She longed to

touch the crystals but everyone was watching her so she kept her hands at her sides.

Thane stood on a platform wearing a purple robe. He spoke sharply to his mother. Bruna gestured wildly and scowled at Sara. Panic tightened in Sara's chest but she fought it back. This was only a dream anyway.

She could tell that woman to eff off.

Then she would wake up, working for her shithead boss and living in her tiny apartment.

She squared her shoulders and walked toward him on steps that looked like granite. She would never have the nerve to do this in her waking life.

"Is something wrong?" she said.

She smiled at Thane's mother. He shook his head.

Sara hated to be the center of attention, and her hands shook when he took firm hold of them.

He looked at his mother. She shook her head at her then stiffly stepped off the platform. Some onlookers gasped.

"What is happening?" she said.

"We are joining," he said. "You chose me."

He let go of her hand and lifted her chin so she had to look at him.

"Yes."

Murmurs of approval hummed through the crowd.

"But your mother—I'm guessing she doesn't approve."

He kept hold of her chin.

"Does it make a difference?" she said.

He looked puzzled.

"Does it change our joining?" she said.

"Not for me," he said.

"Yes." She smiled into his amazing green eyes. "I will join with you."

Whatever that meant.

Her mother's favorite expression, "in for a penny, in for a pound," came to mind.

He kissed her then, probing her lips with his tongue, seeking entry. She opened her lips. He tasted like mint. The crowd roared, and he deepened the kiss, plunging his tongue in and out like the sex she remembered in her dreams.

He broke off the kiss and pressed his forehead to hers.

"No dream, Sara." He lifted her into his arms as if she weighed nothing and carried her off the platform.

"What is this place?" she said.

He carried through rooms gleaming with what looked like amethyst crystals and gold under the shining pink sky.

"The Golden City," he said. "We live under your earth sea, near New Zealand."

They came to a chamber with soft cushions and a shallow pool.

"How is the sky pink under the ocean?" Sara said.

"How is the sky blue above the sea?" he said. He set her on the edge of a shallow pool. "For practice," he winked.

He shucked off his robe and stood wearing only a loincloth. She couldn't take her eyes off him. He smiled, knelt beside her, and unfastened the gown she wore. She shrugged out of it and started to cover herself, but he took gentle hold of her chin.

"No, Sara."

He took her face in his hands. She pressed her mouth into his palm.

Best dream ever.

"No dream," Sara."

"How do you know what I'm thinking?"

"In the sea, we have to talk without words," he said.

"Really?" To test it, she silently commanded him to take off his loincloth. He stood and removed it. *'Kiss me,'* she said silently. He raised an eyebrow at her. She tried once more. *'Please kiss me. I have to taste you and find out is this is real.'*

He stepped into the shallow water, which lapped his magnificent abs, took hold of her waist, and pulled her in.

"I'm afraid," she said out loud before he fused his mouth to hers.

His hand drifted down to her smooth mound and his thumb caressed the bundle of nerves there. She was lost to everything but the taste of his mouth and her impending orgasm. Her terror of water receded like the ocean tide.

The starburst came then, and she was boneless in his arms. He lifted his mouth from hers and he held her back so she was stretched out face up in the water. He murmured soft words she didn't understand and pinched her skin near her hipbone, keeping one hand firmly underneath her back. He kissed her again hard and possessively. Tingles started near her waist, traveled through her feminine core, down her legs to the tips of her toes.

"Sara," Thane called her name in deep, melodic tones.

She stretched out and opened her eyes.

Her legs had vanished. She stared at the emerald green and purple fishtail that she unfurled in the shallow pool. He smiled at her, fingering her emerald necklace and caressing her breasts. He stood in the water on corded, muscled legs like pillars.

"But how?" Her voice sounded far away to her own ears. "I don't swim."

"Yes, love, you do."

He kissed her again and pulled them both under the water. She opened her eyes. He had taken sea form. His tail unfurled in shades of midnight blue and sunset orange.

She was breathing, she realized, under water.

He grasped her hand, and she moved at his side through the shallow pool for forty feet. They surfaced. He let go of her hand and set her on the side of the pool so her tail dangled in the water. She fluttered her fin, giggled, and then frowned when she saw Thane standing on his legs.

"Don't you like your sea form, love?"

"I love it, but I'm like this and you're—how will we—" She shut her eyes in embarrassment.

He palmed her breasts and then pulled on her nipples. She groaned.

"How will we what, love?"

She opened her eyes. His green eyes were lit with mischief.

Convinced she was dreaming, she spoke out loud. "You have a New Zealand accent. Do the kiwis say shagging?"

He threw back his head and laughed before he claimed her mouth in a gentle kiss. His tongue dueled with hers, and she felt the tingling again, then her human feet, legs and feminine core. His hand covered her mound.

"Joining, Sara. In the Golden City. We say joining."

"You change your sea form when you want, but you change me. Is that how it works?"

"For now," he said.

Drops of water glistened on the golden skin on his smooth, hard chest and she wanted to lick it off. But she wanted answers, too.

"Your mother, she doesn't want us to be together. Why?"

He sighed and hoisted himself out of the water. She couldn't tear her eyes away from his toned body and swallowed hard. He was what Becky would call sex on a stick.

What did he want with her, Sara Watson, from Clarkston, Michigan?

"Mum will come around," he said.

"But—" Sara said.

He caressed her bottom lip with his thumb.

She opened her mouth, drew his thumb inside, and sucked hard, remembering he liked that from a previous dream. He shut his eyes then stood, pulling her to her feet, then swung her into his arms.

"No dream, Sara."

"My boyfriend's mother hates me."

He strode through winding crystal corridors into a chamber filled with plush purple cushions and food arranged on small stone plates. Veins of gold ran through the walls.

He slid her out of his arms, her breasts flush against his chest. He looked frustrated.

"Not boyfriend, Sara, we are joined."

She caressed his smooth cheek. "I don't understand."

He raked his fingers through his hair. "I'm making a mess of this."

She lifted on tiptoe to kiss him. She wanted, needed, to ease his distress and please him. She ran her hand up and down his rigid shaft. He shuddered and pulled her down onto the cushions.

"You're mine Sara," His erection pressed against her slit, damp with her arousal. "This will hurt the first time, love." He pushed into her slowly. "Not like our dreams. We are joining for real."

He pressed his thumb on her clit and brought her to quick release. She screamed his name. He breached her hymen quickly then stilled as she adjusted to his thickness.

"Is this different for you, too?" she whispered. "Than it was in my—our—dreams?"

He surged inside her, hitting her G-spot. "Yes, love, even better, a different dimension, more sensation." He thrust deeper. "I can't take this slow."

He moved her necklace aside and bit into the sensitive spot on the tendon between her neck and shoulder. She wrapped her legs around his waist, taking him deeper. He groaned and thrust harder. She felt the cloudburst building. He hit her G-spot again.

"Now, Sara."

She tried to hold back, afraid she would open her eyes in her twin bed, in her apartment.

He slammed into her. "Come for me, love."

She came apart, screaming his name, before she sank into oblivion. She opened her eyes and stared at the elevator walls.

She sat on the floor, her back against the wall, alone. Her coffee-soaked skirt stuck to her thighs. She looked at her purse and sack lunch on the floor next to her. The elevator had stopped between the seventh and eighth floors.

Had she hit her head? She felt her scalp for an injury but she felt nothing. She felt something around her throat and looked in amazement at an emerald necklace. She hid it under her blouse and pushed the button for the ground floor.

She was taking a sick day. She had well and truly lost her mind.

Chapter 3

Thane paced the marble and gold floor of the Great Hall, trying to reason with his mother and Ronan, the male she joined with after his sire was killed trying to free a pod of dolphins trapped when a volcano erupted in the great depths. Ronan held sway with the Ruling Council of the Golden City and his mother held great sway with Ronan.

And Bruna did not approve of his joining with Sara, although Calista had foreseen their union in the amethyst crystals.

"She is human, son, and she is afraid of water," Bruna said.

"She will get over that, Mother," he said. "I will teach her."

"She will not agree to be altered so she can bear your babies," Bruna sneered.

"She will."

"She will have to give up life under a blue sky," Ronan said. "Does she know this?"

"She returned before I could tell her," he said. He balled his hands into fists. "I must go back above the waves to her."

"It does not make sense, your feeling for this human," Bruna said.

He glared at his mother. Ronan was a mere shadow of his sire, Zuke, and was appointed as an advisor to the council by a sheer fluke.

"It's never been done before, joining with a human female," Bruna said.

"Not here, but it has happened in other cities in the Coalition," Thane said.

"Has she used spoken words to say she lives for you?" Bruna said. "She gave you her virgin's blood. But that means nothing to human females in these times."

"You went into my private chamber?" Thane roared.

"Bruna." Ronan held his hand on her shoulder. "Thane, you may go back to her after fourteen rotations of the outer earth, during the Solstice. But she must return with you willingly, not in the throes of joining." He stared at his webbed feet.

"I can't wait that long." Thane longed for Sara and felt physically ill when she slipped through the veil, away from him. "Mother, you could give me a pass," he said.

Those in the Golden City and the other cities under the sea had two chances during the earth's revolution around the power source to slip through the dimension, through earth time and space, and walk under the blue or gray sky on the earth's surface. Blood relatives could gift their pass to one another.

Ronan used his passes to travel with the council twice a year but Bruna never went with him and had no desire to venture out of the Golden City after Thane's sire, Zuke, had perished in the depths.

And humans could travel most easily through the sea or the veil during the longest or shortest day of the earth's rotation.

"Mum?" Thane softened his voice and stood before her.

Zuke's death so long ago had changed his mother from a laughing, adventurous, happy mate and mother to a deeply hurt and distrustful female who gritted her teeth and spoke of nothing but duty. She tried to over-manage her only offspring's life.

His aunt slipped into the chamber and sat his mother's side. She patted Bruna's arm. Calista loved to travel through the seas and dimensions and had used her allotted passes.

"Bruna, remember when you joined with Zuke," Calista said.

"I can't." Bruna shook her head. Ronan stepped away. "If I did, I could no longer draw breath," she said. "Thane's joining with her is fraught. I will—I must spare him."

"You can't." Calista kissed his mother's cheek and sang tones and words their mother had sang to him when he was still learning to use his fins. "He is determined," she whispered.

Bruna nodded and extended her hand toward Thane. She murmured the sacred Sanskrit words, and Thane squeezed her hand in thanks.

⁂

Sara dropped her purse on her dresser and stepped out of her skirt. Nobody had seen her as she ran out of the building. She would lay down then call a doctor. Her dreams, now hallucinations, were not anywhere in the realm of normal.

She stripped off her blouse and remembered Thane's touch on her arms and shoulders. She fingered the emerald-like necklace, wondering why she didn't remembering buying it. It was real and so was Thane. Others had seen him and talked to him.

But what about the rest of it?

She took off her bra and palmed her breasts the way he had under the pink sky during her hallucination.

What would the doctor say? Would she be committed? Would her father have to sign papers?

She pulled on a tank top, grabbed some sweat pants, started to pull them up, and gasped. Her panties were stained with blood. She'd ended her period last week.

Her chest tightened like a vise, and she couldn't breathe. She pressed some toilet tissue between her thighs it came away brownish red. Roaring sounded in her ears, but she heard something pounding and realized someone was at her front door.

"Sara?"

It was Thane.

Sara's chest seized. She gasped for air.

"Open the door, love, please."

She sobbed, in the full throes of panic.

"Love, please, turn the lock."

Darkness threatened to engulf her. She gripped her door knob with sweaty hands.

"Love, touch your necklace. I know you're wearing it. You can't take it off."

She did and the blackness receded.

"Open the door, Sara." He sang the words and she turned the locks with shaking fingers.

He burst through the door and swept her in his arms.

"I know you're confused, love."

She broke away from him and stood before him in her tank top, sans bra, and her panties stained with her blood.

"There's something you have to know about me, Thane. I'll likely be committed. They'll have to call my father, so it will take a while. He lives in Florida. I'm delusional and probably sick—female stuff. But I'm hallucinating." She lifted her necklace. "I don't even remember buying this. And you're in my hallucinations. It used to be I only dreamed of you. But now—trust me, you don't need my shit. Thanks for checking on me. You should go. I need to call Florida—my father."

He hauled her into his arms and kissed her like he was starved for her. He took hold of her waist and lifted her so she hung in his arms. Jagged edges inside her clicked into place, and she felt whole and sane.

He eased her legs around his waist and tore his mouth away from hers to rain kisses on her nape.

"Where's your bed, love?" he said.

Her apartment was tiny and consisted of four rooms, a kitchen, living room, bathroom, and bedroom. She thought of her twin bed and groaned. She pointed to her bedroom.

"It's small," she said. "We both won't fit."

He dropped her next to the bed and peeled off her tank top then her panties. He stared at the stained fabric then held it to his heart.

"You honor me, love," he said. He kept hold of her

panties as he pulled off his jeans and polo shirt then his loincloth. "I'm real, Sara." He pulled her against him. She ached for his touch. "This is real."

He eased them on the bed so she was sheltered in his arms.

"Sleep, Sara." She could feel his erection.

"Sleep?" She lifted her eyes to his. His hand strayed to her slit, damp with her juices. He smiled at her tenderly.

"I was rough with you for your first time. Sleep now."

"But why are we naked?" she asked.

He nestled her into his chest so she could feel the steady beat of his heart. "Nothing between us, Sara, ever."

She inhaled the essence of the sea that was him and shifted her leg against his hard, muscled body. She sighed and willed herself to fall asleep, back to her dreams of him under the pink sky.

※

She felt something move under her and sat up, sliding off her bed and landing on her butt on the floor next to her twin bed. He was naked in her bed, in the glorious flesh. She stood and touched his lean stomach.

Holy hell. He was real.

Her chest tightened up and she moved to the kitchen, naked.

Do something normal.

She made some coffee, used the last of the cream in her empty fridge, and put some bread in her toaster.

Did he eat? And what?

She remembered seeing plates of food in the chamber in her hallucination that he insisted was real. She looked at the fish clock, she picked up at a tourist shop in Ybor City when she was visiting her father in Florida, that hung over her butcher block table.

She'd slept nearly fourteen hours straight. She had to get into the office. Today was payday. She only had $20 in her checking account, and her rent and car payment were due. She shoved the toast in her mouth, laughing as crumbs fell on her breasts. She brushed them off into the sink and gulped her coffee, burning her mouth.

She had to rush. Doug was pissed at her already.

She turned toward her bathroom and collided with Thane's rock hard chest.

He took hold of her waist. "Slow down, love."

"You smell like heaven." The words flew out of her mouth before she could stop them. He took hold of her chin and kissed her. She sucked on his tongue, and he groaned. He lifted her and she wrapped her legs around his waist. He pulled his lips from hers.

He walked them toward her bathtub. "Let's have a soak."

She giggled. Her tub was small and she barely fit her five foot six inch body. He easily stood half a foot taller. "I don't have time. I have to get to the office. We both won't fit anyway."

"Hmmm." He turned on the faucet, closed the drain, then lifted her into the tub. He stepped in behind her and lowered them so he was sitting up and her back was against him.

"We have time." He squeezed her citrus scented shower gel into his hands then washed every inch of her. "You're working with me on a special project, remember, love. Time is different under the sea," he said. He rubbed her nipples and she moaned.

"But I have to get my check and go to the bank," she said.

His hand cupped her sex and his thumb massaged her throbbing clit. "I need this, Sara—the soak and you."

He sucked hard on her neck and she came apart screaming his name. She felt boneless in his arms. His erection pressed against her backside. She turned in his arms and stroked his hard shaft. She smiled into his impossibly green eyes.

"If I could breathe under water, I'd return the favor."

His eyes sparkled and he fingered her necklace. "You can, love."

He kissed her then and she was lost to everything but his taste. He pressed her hipbone and she felt the familiar tingling, then her tail unfurled.

Thane gently guided her to his cock, and she sucked hard. He eased in and out of her mouth. Spurts of warm liquid shot into the water and down her throat before she realized her head was under the water.

Thane took hold of her shoulders and lifted her head so it rested on his chest.

"That was beyond amazing, love. Have you done that before?"

Did she detect a note of jealousy?

"No, never," she said.

It seemed gross before. But, with Thane, it was different; she was different.

She wiggled her green and purple tail. "I love this. But how am I like this and you're not? And how often do you have to soak? And—"

He gripped her chin and kissed her hard. She felt the tingles and her feet, legs, and feminine core returned. He cupped her smooth mound.

"In the Golden City, you would be smooth here, always, if you say yes."

"Say yes to what?"

He sighed and took hold of her necklace. "I have two weeks before we go back. It's a lot to explain. And you want to go to your office."

He set her away from him and stepped out of the tub. She quickly washed her hair then dried it, letting it fall into the natural wave she hated. She glanced in the mirror and gasped.

Holy hell.

Two pink spots of color stained her cheeks and her eyes had never looked so blue. She smoothed on pink lip balm and applied a bit of mascara to her lashes. She resisted the urge to scrape her brown hair into her usual ponytail. She pulled on thigh-high stockings and a skinny black pencil skirt she'd found with Becky in a thrift shop. She'd never had the nerve to wear it before because she thought it made her butt look fat.

She found a fitted white silk blouse she had been saving for a special occasion. It was sheer but the matching skin-toned underwear she'd bought on sale at Victoria Secret made it work.

She found some stupid high—what Becky called fuck-me—heels, and she was ready.

He kept a firm hand on her arm as they made their way to her office. Her paycheck was in her top desk drawer. Doug had attached a sticky note to it.

See me ASAP!!

Crap.

Thane wore a pair of charcoal gray dress slacks and a light blue dress shirt. His golden skin was visible through his open shirt collar. Where and how had he gotten a change of clothes?

Before she could ask him, Doug poked his puffy, bloated face into her office. "Thane, you got a minute, mate?" He glared at her. She shivered.

Thane rolled his eyes when Doug said "mate" and winked at her as he left.

Becky bounded into her office as soon they left and clicked the door shut.

"Spill it, girlfriend. Stand up."

Sara did.

"I love this." Becky eyed her outfit. "You look amazing. Word is the hot investor specifically asked for you."

Sara smiled. "I know, right?"

"Even without his accent, he's sex on a stick," Becky said.

Sara felt her blush to the roots of her hair.

"Holy hell, Sara," Becky gasped. "You gave up your V card—about damn time. We are so going for drinks." She glanced at her phone and sighed. "I've to get back." She lowered her voice. "Cover your ass around Doug. I heard him ask Lynn to email him all the employee files you put together. I don't know what's up with that, but I'll let you know if I hear anything else."

Becky left then and Sara opened her email. She had ten from Doug.

Shit. They were all stupid questions that had no bearing on anything or reminders on how she was supposed to do things that she had done in the first place. Her chest seized up.

Thane's deep melodious words floated in her head.

'*Breathe, love, breathe.*'

She had just stopped her heart from racing when she had another thought. If her hallucination was real, as he insisted it was, he hadn't used a condom.

She did some quick math.

Holy hell.

Blackness took hold. She put her head on her desk and tried to center her thoughts on her mother.

'*Let it go*,' her mother's voice urged.

Her mother was right. Sara should be fine.

Doug came into her office alone, moved around her desk, and stood crowding her. She fingered her necklace and backed her chair away from him.

"Whatever you were *doing* for Thane is finished," he sneered. He put an emphasis on doing. "He's gone, some emergency."

Sara forced herself to take slow, even breaths. Doug put his hand on her shoulder.

Inappropriate.

She shivered.

"This is the way it's going to be," he said. He squeezed her shoulder. "You work with me on what I tell you to."

Doug's cell phone rang. "Shit," he said. He moved away from her. "We'll talk later," he said as he left her office.

Sara fought back panic. She chanted her mother's words over and over until a text came through on her cell phone. It was a number she'd never seen.

~ I'll be back, love.

Chapter 4

Thane's control hung by a thread. The council, at Ronan's insistence, prompted by his mother, had summoned him through the dimensions back to the Golden City. Because he had not been touching Sara when the summons came, he slipped through the veil alone. All he'd been able to do was transmit her a message electronically.

A typhoon had ravaged the place the humans called the Philippines and those who lived in the Golden City were charged with checking the depths and restoring the ecosystem in various sectors.

Dina stood next to his mother in the Great Hall. Thane and Dina had learned their sea fins together and his mother had wanted Thane to join with Dina. The two women laughed and Dina glanced at him. Ronan droned through the list of sectors and Thane volunteered to take the one closest to the place the humans called Florida. He remembered Sara's father lived there.

She had to be in the sea so he could bring her back to him. The council revoked all special passes to slip above the waves in times of emergency. But it was possible for Thane to swim to shore and bring her back through the dimensions through underwater pathways.

But he only had until the solstice.

Dina left his mother's side and sauntered toward him. Her blonde hair hung in waves down her back and her blue-green eyes gazed at him hopefully.

"I could go with you."

"No need." He forced himself to smile and longed to look into Sara's blue eyes that seemed to hold the secrets of the sea.

Dina put her hand on his arm and brushed her breasts against him. He removed her hand and stepped away from her. He felt no stirring for her under his loincloth.

"I've looked through the amethyst crystal," Dina said, raising her voice. "Your land mate is afraid of water, terrified. It's hopeless."

Murmurs rang through the Great Hall.

"I'm leaving now," Thane said. He stepped to his mother to say goodbye. He returned her embrace stiffly.

His aunt kissed his cheek and whispered into his ear. "She means to dissolve your joining with Sara," Calista said. "She is afraid that you would lose joy as she did with your sire."

"So she wants that I never know it?" He tried to keep his voice low.

"Yes. She means to spare you."

Thane tried to summon feelings of tenderness toward his mother, but he couldn't. Her misguided actions were motivated by love, but she had to know she couldn't control him.

"I will bring Sara back with me, Mother," he said. "We are joined, and she is mine."

"She is not strong enough," Bruna said. She wouldn't look at him.

"Nothing, Mother, you will do nothing to stop this, or I will sever our bond."

Gasps rang through the Great Hall. He turned toward the cavern that would lead him through the dimensions to Florida.

"I'm coming with you," said Quinn.

Thane and Quinn had rescued pods of dolphins and guided humpback whales out of shipping lanes together on other eco-missions. Quinn was a wicked surfer, and he usually took sectors where he could ride the waves.

"There's no surf in the Keys, Q, and I don't need help," Thane said.

Quinn snorted as they slipped into the channel and took their sea forms.

"You want to bring your human back before solstice,

and you think you can pull it off alone?" Quinn laughed. "Typical. Besides, once Dina figures you're done for—"

Thane looked at his friend to see if he was having him on before they plunged into the depths. He wasn't. "Q, tell her you want her. She thinks she and I are destined. But it's just Bruna yammering."

They adjusted their sight to swim through the dark expanse to the ancient, secret chasm and short cut through the fathoms to the string of land mass the humans named the Florida Keys.

The chasm was risky.

Many sea forms believed that Thane's sire Zuke was crushed to his end in such a chasm from a disturbance to the sea floor in his haste to return swiftly to his mate and son after he restored an ecosystem near the bottom of the earth, near the axis, after a volcano erupted in the depths.

But swimming for long periods of time in the sea posed risks as well. Those who took sea form could live for hundreds of years without the aging process or disease the humans experienced, but life spans were shortened by trauma if sea forms could not return to the healing pools in the under-water cities.

ೲೢೲ

He and Quinn stopped for rest and nourishment in the Crystal City before they continued on. He wanted to use the abundant quartz crystals to transmit a message above the waves.

A male still learning his fins led him to a room filled with clear crystals. "We have one here." The youngster smiled impishly.

"Have what?" Thane said.

"A human. She lived above the waves. Now she's here."

Before Thane could question him further, he scampered off. Thane adjusted the quartz to send Sara his message.

Go to the Keys in Florida, I will come. He frowned and sent it again, adding *love*.

He found Q, and they ate some of the clams and shellfish offered before they thanked the council representative and set on their way.

'*Why her?*' Q's thoughts rippled through the depths.

'*She's mine,*' Thane answered.

☙❧

"Redo them, every one you didn't format the way I showed you. I need them by Monday. And as you know, you're salary, so no extra pay and no comp time since you screwed it up," Doug said. He leered at her and left the office.

Becky came in as soon as he left and shut the door. "What a tool. I looked at those files. The only difference is the way you organized the personal information and made it easier to navigate," she said. "I can do this in two minutes."

"Don't. If he figures out I got IT involved, I'll be in deeper shit than I am now."

"So I'll do it from your computer," Becky said.

Sara's cell phone pinged a message.

~ *Go to the Keys in Florida, love, I will come.*

She was stunned.

Becky snatched Sara's phone out of her nerveless fingers. "Who sent this?"

"Thane."

"Your dad lives in St. Petersburg, right? Go down there and look for a job. Tell dumb ass Doug you have a family emergency." She squeezed Sara's hand. "You know he's trying to fire you, right? You made him look stupid when Thane brushed him off. I'll miss you but I could sublet your place. My roommate is mentally unhinged. I've got to get out of there. I'll just say I'm your roommate. They won't care as long as they get their rent." Becky scrolled on Sara's phone. "Call your dad and I'll book you a flight. There's one to Tampa for just over a hundred bucks. Can your credit card handle it?"

Sara nodded and pulled her credit card out of her wallet. Becky thumbed the information in and printed out a boarding pass on the printer next to Sara's desk.

"You leave in four hours, Detroit Metro. I'll drive you. We'll swing by my place so I can pick up some stuff and tell my whack job roommate I'm out of there. Then we'll get you packed and on that plane. Move over."

Sara stood up and Becky's fingers flew across her the keyboard.

"Files are fixed. Send dumbass an email that you have a family emergency."

Sara did, blinking back tears. She took deep breaths. Things were happening so fast. And if she went with him, would she ever see Becky again?

Becky looked around the office. "Anything you want to take?"

"Just you," Sara said, choking back a sob.

"You know, I've got some time," Becky said. She pulled out her phone and thumbed quickly and something spit out of the printer.

Sara stared at the two boarding passes.

"I used your credit card," Becky said. "We'll settle up later. Let's go, chickie."

✿✿✿

She and Becky sat in Sara's father's living room. Sara's cheeks hurt from trying to keep a smile on her face. Her father, Don, hugged her warmly when they got there and had tears in his eyes when he released her. His wife Renee swooped in and asked him to please fix them all some lemonade, which Sara didn't even like.

Renee talked non-stop, nervous chatter that made Sara's head ache. Becky caught her eye and made a gagging face. Sara giggled at an inappropriate moment in Renee's monologue about a neighbor who was ill, and Renee glared at her.

"I was thinking of something that happened at work, sorry," Sara said.

Her father stayed silent.

"I'll just get a drink of water," Sara said.

She went into the kitchen.

Renee followed, close on her heels. "You make him remember and grieve for her," Renee said.

She looked nothing like Sara's mother who was tall and willowy. Renee was petite and plump in a matronly way.

"You're beautiful like she was. I've seen pictures. He can barely function when he remembers. I love him, dear. I know I make him forget. He's happy here. He talks. He's not like he is now that he sees you. Maybe in time—"

Sara nodded. Being with her father made her heart feel heavy. "We're going to the Keys," she said.

Renee poured ice water from a pitcher in the fridge into her glass.

Sara went back into the living room and sat next to her father. "We're going to Key West, Dad," she said. "Any suggestions?"

He frowned. "You're afraid of the water. It's a long drive across narrow stretches."

"I'm driving," Becky said. "I'll blindfold her if I have to."

Everyone laughed.

"Duvall Street."

༺༻

Becky drove like a demon for six straight hours. Before they left, Becky dragged her into a new-age store near the beach in what Renee called St. Pete. The store was filled with crystals, fragrant oils, tarot card decks, and books. Psychics gave readings and Becky insisted they both have one. While they waited, Becky bought Sara some lavender oil and an amethyst crystal. The salesgirl said both had calming effects, and Becky said it was either that or a blindfold when they drove down the turnpike, surrounded by the water.

Becky had her tarot card reading first. Sara heard tidbits of Becky's reading. Amy, the psychic, used the phrase "get out of your own way," often and said if Becky started her own consulting business, she would be very successful.

Becky hovered nearby when it was Sara's turn. Amy had warm brown eyes and snow white hair that fell in waves around her youthful face and gasped when Sara sat down.

She fought back the tightness in her chest and clutched the amethyst crystal.

"Your necklace. May I see it?"

Sara pulled it out from under her T-shirt. She'd kept it covered since Thane left. She couldn't find the catch to take it off. She leaned across the table, closer to Amy, so she could get a better look.

"Wow. Your friend." Amy lowered her voice. "Do you trust her? She's listening, I think."

"With my life."

"Okay, then," Amy said. "Your necklace." She took a deep breath and shut her eyes.

"Do I need to shuffle the cards?" Sara said.

"No. There is a woman with her hands on your shoulders. She has the same color hair and eyes you do, and she sends you so much love. Your mother?"

Sara kept quiet, refusing to reveal information the self-professed psychic could exploit.

"She's passed, a disease in her pancreas," Amy said.

Sara swallowed hard and nodded.

"She says for you not to worry. You'll undergo a procedure, if you wish it, in a different place so you will bear many children safely. I keep seeing pink above you. Again, this is your choice to stay there. Are you in a relationship?"

Sara shrugged. "I met someone."

"I see water and—" Amy's eyes went wide, "a male." She seemed to choose "male" carefully. "His name is Thorn, or something that starts with Th. Your mother says he's your true destiny, if you have courage. He's not like us—I mean like me and your friend are. You are becoming like him. You will be the same as him if you choose to be. Your necklace denotes high rank. It won't be easy for you." Amy shuddered. "But your love for each other—" She shut her eyes again. "The essence is the strongest I've ever felt. Again, you have a choice to stay, your mother says. She knows you are afraid. Your dreams are real, she says. Wow," she said, opening her eyes. "I've been doing this for a while. That was incredible. I've never channeled anything like this. It's been an honor."

Becky stayed quiet until they got back in their rental car. "Holy shit, Sara. You want to tell me what's going on?"

"I will," Sara said. After we get there, okay?"

They peeled down Highway 1, and Sara splurged on a hotel as close to Duval Street as they could get.

She'd had no more texts. She and Becky drank mojitos at an outside table in a restaurant with a wooden mermaid hanging over the bar and watched the cars and people crawl up the street. Two guys in polo shirts bought them a second round. Becky leaned across the table. "Spill it, Sara."

"Shouldn't we eat?" Sara said. "I'm a lightweight with the hard stuff."

"Good. We'll eat after," Becky said. "Talk to me."

Sara took a long sip of her second mojito. "I dreamed of him—Thane—smoking hot dreams, Beck. Then there he was in our office. I thought I was crazy. I still think so." She downed the rest of her drink and stared at the mermaid. "He's like that." She pointed to it. "And I'm like that too when I'm with him and he wants me to be. He lives under the sea where the sky is pink and veins of gold run through the crystal hallways and caverns. And his mother hates me."

She hiccupped. The room was spinning. She slurred her words. "Start the paperwork to have me committed. You'll need my dad's signature."

"Water, please," Becky said to the passing waiter. "And chicken wings and loaded potato skins, fast as you can, please."

The two guys in polo shirts staggered over to them. The guy in the yellow polo shirt put his arm around Sara's shoulders. She stiffened and took a long sip of the ice water the waiter slammed down in front of her. She tried to wiggle away from polo shirt, but he clamped his sweaty hand down tighter.

"Relax, baby." He said his name, Brad, or Brian.

She couldn't remember and she wouldn't ask him to repeat it.

The waiter brought the chicken wings and potato skins and Brad/Brian helped himself to a wing.

Becky winced. "We're waiting for our boyfriends," she said. "But thanks for the drinks."

The guy in the orange polo shirt stared at Becky's boobs.

"B—Bullshit," Brad/Brian said. "We just want to have a little fun. We're harmless." He put his sweaty hand on Sara's thigh, which made her instantly sober.

"Please don't," she said, moving her leg away from his hand.

Becky had crossed her arms across her chest.

"We'll leave when they get here. We have nobody to talk to and we're bored." He clamped his hand back on her shoulders.

"Sh—show me those beautiful titties," orange polo shirt said to Becky. "You owe me that much for these freaking drinks."

"I owe you?" Becky shrieked. "For this?" She picked up her drink and dumped it on his lap.

Sara stood up and shook off Brian/Brad's creepy touch. "The wings are on us." She picked up her purse and the heavy plate of potato skins. "Really, we're waiting. And her boyfriend will beat the shit out of you. So leave."

Sara moved to a table across the restaurant with Becky on her heels. The assholes devoured the chicken wings like they hadn't eaten in days.

Steve, their waiter, brought them fresh waters. "I'm not charging you for the wings, I'll just add it to dumb and dumber's bill. They're so hammered, they won't notice. I was just about to cut them off. Sorry about that."

Sara smiled into Steve's eyes. They were chocolate brown. He was tall and lean and real.

"Is it true?" he said. "Do you have a boyfriend?"

"Husband, actually," a deep voice behind her said.

It was Thane. He rested his hands on the nape of Sara's neck.

A hot guy with turquoise eyes and streaky brown hair stood next to Becky, whose mouth gaped open.

Chapter 5

"Husband?" Becky said.

The hot guy deftly slid half the potato skins onto a plate and picked it up. "Let's give them a minute, darlin'."

Becky stared at her. Sara nodded, and Becky and hot guy moved to a clean table several feet away.

"Thanks, Steve." She smiled at the waiter. Was she goading Thane? Steve winked at her then left.

Thane wore a T-shirt, surfer shorts, and flip-flops, nearly identical to hot guy's.

"He's my friend and his name is Quinn," Thane said. Damn. She'd forgotten he could read her thoughts.

Thane was as hot as she remembered. He sat down

next to her and tugged on her emerald necklace, bringing her face close to his. He smelled like she remembered, what he had told her was ambergris in her dreams.

He glanced at Steve and set his mouth in a thin hard line. "Miss me?" he said, anger creeping in to his voice.

He didn't wait for an answer. He kissed her. His lips hardened and he plunged his tongue inside her mouth until she forgot everything but his taste and let him dominate her.

She went boneless in his arms. He lifted his mouth, stared into her eyes, and seemed satisfied with what he saw there.

"You're mine, love," he growled, glaring at Steve.

He nearly pulled her onto his lap, picked up a potato skin, and held it to her lips. She ate it, and felt more clearheaded. He fed her again and she looked nervously around the restaurant, but nobody was watching them. Becky sipped her water and laughed at whatever Quinn said. Sara looked at Steve, who was settling the bill with the polo shirt boys. She saw Steve and Quinn's male beauty but she only wanted Thane. But he had disappeared—into thin air.

"You left," she said.

"I was called," he said. "I will be called again."

He fed her another potato skin and lifted her hair to nuzzle her neck and inhaled deeply. The tightness in her chest that never seemed to leave her dissolved. She sighed.

"I will always come back unless I am harmed."

The tightness took hold again. "Like a soldier," she said.

"Not for conflict," he said. "We, the Council of Cities, have held peace for three thousand of your years."

"Our years?"

He fed her again. "Time is different in the Golden City."

"How old are you?"

He grinned. "Beats me."

"I think I need another drink," she said.

Becky's laughter rang through the restaurant.

"Wow. Your friend must be a comedian. She hardly ever laughs that hard."

She remembered the different language he spoke in the Golden City.

"He's a cut up," he said. He fed her the last potato skin.

"How many languages do you speak?"

She caressed the line of his jaw. He shrugged. "Land languages of English and the words that come from Latin." He traced lazy circles on her wrist over her pulse point. "Too lazy to learn the Slavic or African words."

Women in short-shorts with Barbie doll figures sauntered into the restaurant and openly ogled Thane and Quinn, ignoring the polo shirt jerks. One with long platinum blonde hair flipped it off her shoulder and tried to catch Thane's eye, although Sara was virtually in his lap.

When that didn't work, she walked up to them, ignored Sara, and leaned over, giving him a view of her ample cleavage, which Sara thought had to be fake.

"You surf, right?" The blonde touched his arm.

Sara wanted to punch her in her perfectly made up face.

The blonde didn't wait for an answer. "Could you come with me to a store down the street?" She pressed her boob against his shoulder. "I need help picking out a board."

The surf in the Keys was sporadic and mostly non-existent and Sara said as much.

The blonde ignored her. "Please," she pressed closer to him and pouted her lips. She looked dismissively at Sara. "I'll make it worth your while." She tugged on his arm.

Sara saw the blonde's fake fingernails on his skin. A red haze clouded her vision, and she could feel her heart pound.

"No." He used the tone he'd used with his mother. "I'm with my wife."

Sara stood then. A line from one of her mother's favorite movies, *Coal Miner's Daughter*, sprang to her lips. "You want to keep that arm, get it off my husband," she said, but in her flat Midwestern tones.

The blonde staggered back on her high-heeled sandals. Her eyes narrowed to slits and she looked pointedly at Sara's bare left hand.

"Didn't see a ring. Whatev."

The polo shirt guys couldn't take their eyes off the blonde. Brad/Brian staggered over. "I'll go, baby." He reeked of rum. "He deserves the bitch. She's a frigid cock tease."

Thane's fist connected with Brad/Brian's jaw and knocked him out cold. A bald, red-faced man ran toward them. "Out, all of you, now."

The orange polo shirt guy roused his friend, and Sara grabbed her purse. Steve laughed, winked, and saluted her. Thane wrapped an arm around her waist and steered her outside into the throng of people on the street.

"You know that guy?" His voice was clipped, his New Zealand accent as strong as he had ever noticed. "He winked at you."

She saw a tic in his cheek she'd never seen before. He looked around and pulled her into a narrow alley. He took hold of her waist and walked her back against a wooden fence then lifted her as though she was weightless and fit her torso to his.

He took her mouth then, plundered it really, and she forgot the crowd, Becky, the blonde bimbo and everything except him. He dragged his mouth away and she hung in his arms.

Why did she love it so much when he went all alpha male and dominated her like this? She was wet, for God's sake. And her nipples stuck out in pouty points.

"You're mine, love. No one touches you but me."

He let her down so her sensitive nipples rubbed against his chest. His hand covered her sex, and he pushed a finger easily inside her shorts to her wet slit. "This is mine, Sara."

He kissed her again, muffling her scream when he quickly brought her to orgasm. He held her against him till she could find her feet. She slid her hand beneath his shirt and caressed his rock hard abs then his erection.

"That goes both ways." She stared into his amazing green eyes, the same color as the emerald necklace she wore when the sunlight caught it just right.

"I'm yours as long as you draw breath, love," he said.

She pumped her hand up and down his cock, feeling the pre-cum on his tip.

"Not here, love."

She pulled her hand away reluctantly and licked the moisture from her palm.

He shut his eyes and groaned then rested his damp forehead against hers, breathing like he had just sprinted a mile.

"Sara?" Becky and Quinn stood at the entrance to the alley.

"It's going to rain, mate, in about twenty minutes," Quinn said. He turned a devastating smile on Becky. "Could we go back to your place, darlin'?"

He took a tight hold of her hand as they trudged through the throng of people to Sara and Becky's hotel.

༈༺༈

Thane was determined to keep her within touching distance, in case the council summoned them and he and Quinn slipped through the dimensions back to the depths. If he were not physically touching her, she would remain on land as she had before. Then she would have to start the journey into the depths alone, in peril, and she was terrified of the sea. He would, he must, spare her that terror. He knew she loved her sea form. She would learn to love the depths—in time. He would go slowly with her.

They got inside the lobby just as the rain started. They went to her room and Quinn opened the sliding door to the balcony. He and Quinn stood indoors and inhaled the rain soaked air deeply, replenishing the reserves they would need to keep their land forms until the solstice in two days.

Since they were so close to the salt water, the rain on their skin could prompt their sea forms against their will.

He knew he had to talk to her about what her life would be with him in the Golden City. He wanted her with him joyfully, not terrified, with full understanding, not in her dream state.

Quinn smiled at Becky. "Let's grab a drink, darlin'."

Becky looked at her. Sara nodded and they left them.

"I only booked one room. It was expensive," she said. She worried her bottom lip.

He peeled off his shirt and sat on the bed with his

back against the pillows. He spread his legs, indicating that she should sit between them. "We have to talk, love. There's so much I have to tell you."

She sat so her back rested against his chest and nuzzled her soft cheek against his shoulder. He stroked her hair and fingered her necklace. "We are joined, love, and I want you with me always. Do you want that, too?"

She nodded.

"You would be my wife in the Golden City and take your sea form in the depths. You would grow my seed and give birth if you want."

She twisted around to look at him. "I do."

Confusion clouded her beautiful turquoise eyes. He cupped her chin. "It would be like you dreamed," he said. "You'd live under the pink sky and you would be altered so you wouldn't miss your blue sky or sunshine as much. And we can come back to land four times in each of your years. But we won't age, not like here and that would raise suspicion and possible harm to those that live in the depths."

"So I could come back at first to see my dad and Becky but not later," she said.

"There is risk in coming back, but most of us do," he said. "The healing mineral pools in the Golden City keep us free of disease but we *can* be harmed, then we perish. My sire, Zuke, was called to free great pods of dolphins trapped by a volcanic explosion in the depths and he never returned. So my mother never leaves. She was different before."

"You left," she murmured.

He sighed. "I was summoned back through the dimensions, and since you weren't with me, you stayed here. It's easiest for sea forms to make the journey on the solstice."

"That's on Thursday," she said. She looked puzzled. "Why me?" she whispered. "You could have someone who looks like that blonde bimbo in the bar."

He nuzzled her neck and chuckled. "You will be altered. You could be like that if you want."

She moved away from him. "No," she yelled. "If that's what you want—"

He covered her beautiful lips with his hand. He winced. "Bad joke, love. I want you, Sara, only you. I saw you in the crystals and I couldn't hold back. I took you in your dreams."

"It was mutual."

He took hold of her waist. "You're mine. You were made for me. I know I sound like a conceited jerk, but it's true. And I'm yours, too, if you'll have me."

"Yes, yes, yes." She turned fully in his arms. "So I can't get pregnant until they do something to me in the Golden City?"

"Yes," he said.

She rubbed against his erection. He lifted her shirt

and unhooked her bra to suckle her breast. She arched toward him and moaned.

※

"Lock that door," she said.

He slid the lock, keeping hold of her and they fell back on the bed. She wrapped her legs around his waist. He nudged his erection in her wet slit and slid inside her sheath, hitting her sweet spot. She sighed.

How could she live without this? But how could she live forever in such a different place?

He pounded into her and she met him thrust for thrust. He hit her sweet spot again, and she came hard before he emptied himself inside her. He pulled out of her and she watched his magnificent ass as he strode into the bathroom. He returned with a washcloth and gently cleaned her.

"Have you been joined with others?"

He nodded. "Before I saw you in the crystals."

"Will I meet them? Will they hate me?" She traced circles on his chest with a trembling finger. He brought her hand to his mouth and kissed her palm.

"No, love. They were from the Emerald city and it wasn't joining. We had no connection."

"Emerald City, like the *Wizard of Oz*?"

He looked puzzled.

"*The Wizard of Oz*. The book and movie?"

He shrugged. "Sorry love."

She sat up and smiled. "I'll have to bring you up to speed on pop culture."

"Up to speed, you mean teaching?"

She laughed. "Yes, and idioms, figures of speech, American slang, sayings."

"Got it, love. But they will change. Time is different in the Golden City. We'll learn the new sayings together when we come back."

"Were you with very many women?"

How could she possibly measure up? He had to learn his amazing sexual prowess somehow. She had nobody to compare him too but from what Becky and the girls in her college dorm said, she figured sex with him was off the charts.

"A handful," he said. She noticed the tic near his jaw again. "Sowing my wheat," he said.

She giggled. "Oats, you mean. Sowing your oats or wild oats."

"Got it. I never spilled my seed inside them, only you, Sara."

She lifted her face to kiss him, sucking on his tongue and rubbing herself against his hard cock. He took her slowly, drawing out her release. He pushed her back on the bed, held her wrists captive above her head, and ravished her mouth.

"We go together, love." He found her sweet spot, pressed his thumb against her clit, and pinched her nipple.

She came so hard she saw stars, sobbing his name and how much she loved him.

He held her till she settled down and dozed off.

Chapter 6

She woke to insistent knocking on the door.

"Rack off," Thane said.

"Sara?" It was Becky.

"She needs the loo," Quinn said.

She winced, sure that anyone in the hallway must have heard him.

"I need my suitcase," Becky said. "Sorry."

Thane pulled his shorts on, grabbed a bathrobe the hotel provided, and handed it to Sara. She put it on and he opened the door. She looked at her clothes in a pile on the floor and felt her cheeks flame. She couldn't look at Becky or Quinn.

"Sorry," Becky mumbled. She grabbed her suitcase and went into the bathroom as Quinn flipped the lock latch on the door.

Sara guessed her friend started her period and frowned.

Their cycles were in sync—they laughed about it.

They both craved chocolate and potato chips before they started.

Thane glared at Quinn.

"What you brassed off with, mate? You had time enough for a bonk."

"Rack off," Thane said. He sat on the bed and put his arm around her. She'd gone stiff with nerves.

"What's wrong, love?"

She did some quick math. She was late. She glanced at Quinn. "Later," she said softly.

He said she wouldn't conceive, not without undergoing some procedure under the waves. Nerves likely threw off her cycle. She picked up her clothes and dumped them into her suitcase. Quinn was restless. Becky stuck her head out of the bathroom. "Could you come in here?"

Thane looked uneasy.

"She'll be three feet away," Quinn said. "You've got it bad, mate." He chuckled.

Thane reluctantly let her go. Sara went in to the bathroom and pulled the door shut. It was a tight fit with the humidity.

"I was talking to Quinn. Holy shit, Sara." Becky looked worried. "Are you sure about all this? Quinn told me Thane's mum, I mean mother, is dead set against you. That's why he left before. She wanted him back there. You'll be leaving everything you know, and me." Her voice broke and her eyes filled with tears.

The familiar tightness settled in Sara's chest. "He's the only one I want," she said. "I don't want to live without him."

"He's the only one you've had," Becky said. "You have nobody to compare him to, and you hate the water."

"It's different when he's with me and I'm different," she said.

"Quinn said they go on eco missions a lot," Becky said. "He'll leave you alone with his bitch of a mother."

Sara shuddered and starred at the floor.

"Tell him you need more time," Becky said. "Go back to St. Pete and look for a job. Think this over, please. How do you know you'll be his only wife? What if they—"

"He said I belong to him and that no one else touches me and that he's mine, too."

Becky rolled her eyes. "I get it, Sara, he's sexy as hell. You are putting your life in his hands, under water."

Sara thought of the vast expanse of blue on both sides of the highway on the ride down. Her throat closed up, she couldn't breathe, and her heart thudded.

"Sara, you're white as a sheet," Becky said.

Something clattered outside the bathroom door.

"Shit," Quinn said. "Your mum again."

"Sara, let me in," Thane yelled.

She tried to push the door open.

It was stuck.

"Hurry, love."

Becky and Sara pushed against it with all their might.

"Sara," Thane screamed.

They got the door open.

They were gone.

And the door was still latched from the inside.

"No," Sara wailed.

She curled up on the bed and sobbed.

Becky stepped out on the balcony. "Quit screwing around, you assholes, Sara is upset." They weren't there. "Sara, they probably shimmied down the balcony. I'll check around. Stay here."

Sara couldn't move if she had to. Why did she leave Thane's side when he seemed so uneasy about it? If she could put up with Doug's shit, she could put up with Thane's mother's shit. It was a moot point, now, anyway.

A text pinged on her Smart Phone.

Hope bloomed. Becky must have found them. Sara laughed joyfully and grabbed her phone.

Dolphins, love. Swim tomorrow.

She stared at the words until Becky got back.

"I couldn't find them. This whole thing is shady, hon," Becky said. "You're better off."

"No," Sara barked. "I'm not, Beck. He sent me a text." She handed Becky her phone. "We've got to do one of those dolphin swims tomorrow."

ତେତେତ

"Why, Mother? I will be with her despite your antics," he roared at his mother.

She flinched but her voice stayed steady. "You were needed."

"Quinn could have done it alone."

"Thane," Ronan said.

"She belongs with me," Thane said. "I'll never join with anyone but her. I will be as lonely and bitter as you are, Mother."

Ronan flinched but stayed silent.

Thane pitied Ronan for his love and devotion to a woman who did not love him. Still he pressed on. "I will be an empty shell, like mother, like son."

Ronan stepped away from his mother.

"Ronan," his mother said.

"No," Ronan said. His voice was sharper than Thane ever remembered. "Use the crystal to send her a message. I can only hope she will give you her heart, not scraps of hope," he muttered. "I see you are determined. In that you are like your sire."

Thane stepped to Ronan and put his hand on his shoulder in a gesture of respect he'd never given his mother's mate before. Ronan gripped his arm in acknowledgement. He and Ronan left Bruna weeping silently with Calista at her side.

"The dolphins," Ronan said. "They will know her if she has taken sea form."

"She has," Thane said.

"Take Quinn with you," Ronan said. "Bruna said she is afraid of the sea."

"Not in her sea form, not with me," Thane said.

"Let us hope that is enough," Ronan said. "She will swim with the dolphins a distance before you can reach her, if she understands the intent of the message and if there is no mishap." Ronan said the words calmly and Thane saw his value to the council in his role as advisor.

They reached the quartz chamber, and Ronan placed his hands on his shoulder then left him.

೧೨೮೨

Sara forced air into her lungs as she put the life vest around her neck.

"Sara, this is ridiculous," Becky said. "You're terrified. We don't have to do this."

Sara pulled the straps tight like the instructor had shown them. Their dolphin swim was in a pool beside the ocean. She knew logically that she would have to swim through the open sea to get to Thane and the dolphin swim was not in the sea, though the pool was a few feet away from the Atlantic. But none of the dolphin swims offered a dip in the sea. She had no idea how this would lead her to him, but she knew she had to do it.

"No," she said. 'I'm sick of being afraid. You helped me with that, Beck." She fingered her emerald necklace. "I wouldn't have had the guts to even be here if it wasn't for you."

Becky looked at her doubtfully. "Okay, let's get in the pool. We can stop any time you want."

Sara's throat closed up as she stepped in the shallows. One of the dolphins was next to the instructor. The sea creature seemed to smile at her and the tightness in her throat and chest seemed to dissolve. Becky stared at her.

"I'm okay," Sara said. "Really."

They formed a line. She and Becky were last, since she didn't want to hold anybody up if she got panicky. The dolphins performed a bit on Ben, the instructor's command, swimming up to him to "kiss" his cheek then jumping in the air.

"This one is named Jumper and he loves to show off," Ben said.

Three dolphins were in the pool. Each person was to swim separately to a spot in the deep end, so a dolphin could kiss their cheek, "swim" a short distance holding onto the dolphin, and then have a photo taken. Unbidden,

Jumper swam to her before it was her turn. She petted him gently, and he made a dolphin noise.

Ben was shocked. "That's never happened before. The noise, I mean. He's talking to you."

Ben clapped and blew a whistle and Jumper swam back into formation. She focused on Jumper, which seemed to calm her. Becky took her turn and smiled for the camera with her dolphin, Ada.

It was Sara's turn and Jumper awaited Ben's command as she tentatively made her way to the deep end.

"You okay, hon?" Becky called.

Sara stared at the vast expanse of ocean just beyond the pool, shuddered, and pulled her focus back to Jumper, who seemed to be smiling at her. "Yeah."

She gave the thumbs up and touched her emerald necklace. Jumper came to her, and she turned her cheek so the dolphin could kiss it. She grabbed hold of the dolphin, made their lap around the pool, and stopped for the photo. Jumper made no move to leave her. All the other instructors, dolphins, and people except for her, Becky, Jumper, and Ben were gone.

"You can do a couple more laps if you want. He really likes you," Ben said.

She clung tightly to Jumper. The dolphin swam faster than before and faster than the other dolphins had. Becky called her name. Sara clung tightly to Jumper. The dolphin picked up even more speed and swam toward the open sea.

"Shit," Ben said, just before he blasted his whistle.

Jumper put his nose up, and they flew through the air in an arc over the enclosed area toward the open sea. Sara screamed, partly from fear and partly from joy.

Jumper belly-flopped into the Atlantic. Sara screamed again as Jumper headed farther and farther out into the open sea. She managed to keep her head above the water most of the time. The ocean felt colder and chilled her skin. How long would it take them to raise a search party?

Ben said that Jumper was bred in captivity. Could the dolphin survive in the Atlantic? Would she survive this? Would the rescue boat reach her before Thane could?

She couldn't hear anything over roaring in her ears. Jumper made a small noise then dove briefly underwater. Sara came to understand the dolphin was warning her before he plunged them into the sea. Jumper did this repeatedly, and they swam underwater for longer each time.

The dolphin swam faster underwater. Sara gripped Jumper tighter and tighter with each plunge. Her arms felt like noodles. Jumper made his noise and dove. She held on with all her strength, but it was no use. Her arms fell away, and she bobbed to the surface. Her head was barely out of the frigid water. Her teeth chattered. She couldn't see Jumper. Her throat closed up, and she forced herself to take deep gulps of air.

Were there sharks in these waters? She remembered

a girl who had lost an arm to a shark while surfing who had been a contender on her favorite reality show. She tried to draw courage from that woman's positive spirit.

"Jumper?" she called.

Had the kind-hearted dolphin fallen prey? She couldn't see land anymore but she heard a faint whir of an engine overhead. Was it a helicopter?

She felt a rush under water.

"Jumper," she yelled.

The dolphin nudged at her life jacket. She knew it slowed them down underwater.

She would die for sure without it if she was separated from Jumper again. Or she could die wearing it while she waited to be rescued. Either way, she wouldn't see Thane again. Tears rolled down her cheeks. She felt her flat stomach.

What if she was carrying his baby? He said it wasn't possible. But she was never late.

She wanted her mother, and Thane, and Becky. But she had Jumper.

'*In for a penny…*'

Her mother's soft words. The engine in the sky sounded closer. Her fingers went to the straps on her life vest. They were tight and wet, and she struggled to work them loose. Her chest contracted in panic. She focused on Jumper and took deep, steady breaths. She loosened the straps enough to ease out of the vest and let it go.

Jumper smiled and squawked with joy. Shivering, she grabbed hold of his fins and took a deep breath. They plunged again, and her lungs felt like they would explode. She squeezed the dolphin's fins, and he surfaced. She gasped.

A pod of whales swam in the distance.

Were she and Jumper in danger? She'd never read *Moby Dick* but she knew the general story. Jumper made his diving noise again. When they surfaced, Sara saw a ship quite a distance away and a helicopter overhead.

Her heart hurt.

She would be rescued.

She would never see Thane again.

He would never know the child she might be carrying.

And their child would never know him.

They plunged again. Would their relationship have survived anyway? They were different species—until she agreed to be altered, anyway. She would be leaving her job she worked hard to get, Becky, her father, and everything she knew.

She knew she could come back and see Becky, but Becky would age and she wouldn't.

You hate your job and rarely speak to your father.

Her teeth chattered. How much longer would she last in the cold water? The helicopter hovered and the ship drew closer. If she signaled, she could be rescued soon.

Jumper made a noise so loud it hurt her ears before they dove again.

She wouldn't stop trying to reach Thane, but how much longer could she go on? Would drowning be a pleasant death? She could see her mother again.

A muscle cramp shot up her leg and she opened her mouth in a panicked attempt to draw breath to ease the pain.

Her baby, she had to live for her baby.

She squeezed hard on Jumper's fins, and he surfaced. She tried to draw air into her lungs. Her chest felt like it was on fire. Her leg cramp flared. She winced and put her head on Jumper, trying to breathe through it, when everything went black.

Chapter 7

Quinn and Thane slipped through the cavern and dimension to the Keys.

They both had looked into the amethyst crystals and saw Sara's distress. Quinn took a second look and gasped. He put his hand on his shoulder.

"We may be too late, and the humans mean to rescue her, mate. She has your baby, and she means to live."

They swam swiftly through the depths, pushing their sea forms to their limits after they heard the dolphin's distress wail.

His heart ached, not from exertion but thinking that she would come to harm in the ocean or be taken back to land before they could reach her. If she was rescued, she would attract attention, and if they went on land to be with her, so would he, putting those who lived in the cities in the depths in great peril. And he could only stay on land in human form for two earth rotation before he had to take his sea form or perish.

She could only take the shortcuts through the depths and dimensions in the caverns during the solstice, which was this day.

If she agreed to be wholly altered to her sea form, it would be different.

His mind reeled at the thought of their baby. The elders said conception with humans could only happen if the humans agreed to be altered. It had never happened before in the recorded history of the Golden City.

Did she want their baby? Did the fetus put her in danger, more peril than she was in now at the mercy of the sea?

They heard it then—the dolphin shriek. She was with him and other humans would come. He knew the dolphin was not likely a sea native, or if it was, it was maimed. Humans, to their credit, were known to care for sea forms that were hurt or maimed by fishing nets or ships.

If the humans rescued her, or she chose not to be with him in the depths, their child and she could be in grave danger if the child manifested sea form. He shot through the sea in an intense burst of speed. He surfaced and saw her and the dolphin at a distance. He also saw a ship making its way toward them and heard a machine in the sky drawing closer.

"We need a diversion," said Quinn as he surfaced.

They plunged again. He or Quinn would get captured in any diversion he could think of. That was if she was willing to sink through the depths to be with him. He couldn't let Quinn perish so he and Sara could escape. What sort of happiness would they have, knowing Quinn sacrificed his life force for them?

The dolphin dove underwater again, making his way toward them. What if she lost her grip on the dolphin? She must be tired and cold.

Quinn's words came to him. *'Should we should continue underwater to get closer quicker or surface to see what is happening?*

'Surface,' he answered.

He would lose his mind if he couldn't see her.

The ship was close. He could see the words "Coast Guard" on the side.

"Go to her," Quinn said.

Thane hesitated. The dolphin forcibly shook her off him then circled and jumped over her head in an arc. She wasn't wearing a life vest and the wind had picked up. She struggled against the waves.

"Go to her," Quinn said. "We've got our diversion."

Thane raced to her and grabbed her as her lungs gave out, and she sank underwater. He put his mouth on hers and stroked her hip until she took sea form. She didn't have her sea vision yet but she seemed to know him by touch.

'*Will you come with me, love?*' He sent his words to her. She groped for his hand, pressed it to her stomach, and smiled.

'*Baby*,' she said.

The dolphin screeched. She grabbed hold of Thane, halting their progress.

'*Jumper sounds hurt*,' she said. '*We have to go back.*'

'*Precious heart,*' he said. He maneuvered her so her arms were wrapped around his neck so they could swim faster. '*No, love,*' he answered. '*Quinn is there. He'll do what he can.*'

She pressed her cheek into his neck. He felt her grief for the dolphin. Would she grieve for her life on land?

She could return above the waves if she demanded it. His mother, he was sure, would encourage her. Would his mother ever accept her? Maybe the news of the life he planted that grew in her would soften Bruna's heart.

What would the physicians say? They hadn't believed it was possible. Or was it a lie to keep the species from joining their lives together?

He felt movement behind them and turned to shield her. Sharks would detect human scent.

It was Quinn. '*Dolphin?*' Thane said.

'*They got him—alive,*' Quinn answered.

'*Sharks?*' Thane asked, hoping Sara didn't pick up his thought.

He could feel her fear. It was tempered by determination and love. Was it love for him or love for their baby? She'd cried out words of love in the throes of her orgasm. But did she mean them? And if she did, would it hold up against his mother's coldness in a place so different than what she was used to?

'*Not far.*' Quinn's words came. '*The sharks.*'

Thane knew she needed more air in her lungs. '*I have to stop. Keep going,*' he said.

'*No,*' Quinn answered.

Thane tugged on her arms. She loosened them. He took hold of her emerald necklace and pulled her to face him. '*Kiss me,*' he commanded.

He fused his mouth to hers. He could taste her fear, but she wanted him, too. '*Thank the source of all life.*'

She had enough air but he couldn't break their connection.

Quinn jabbed his shoulder. '*Shark.*'

He tore his mouth from hers. '*Take her.*' The cavern through the dimensions to the Golden City was an earth mile away. And Thane was the better shark fighter, although Quinn hated to admit it.

Quinn handed Thane the small spear he'd carried around his neck, sent a rude word through the waves, and took hold of Sara. Still sea blind, she knew it wasn't

Thane who had hold of her. Her panic rippled through the waves. The shark sensed it and came closer.

'*Go*,' Thane ordered. He bit into his wrist, drawing blood to attract the shark. The predator's snout swam straight toward him.

All who took sea form were trained to fight sharks. The sharks and dolphins were not a food source for those who lived in the depths.

'*We're in.*'

Quinn's words rippled faintly through sea, which meant she was safe in the cavern—far enough away from the dead-eyed predator. Thane gripped Quinn's spear. How had he been so stupid to leave his own spear in the Golden City? Quinn and Sara were vulnerable.

'*Leave*,' he said.

'*No.*' That time Sara answered.

He flicked his tail and the shark went for it. He plunged the spear, aiming for the shark's neck. He speared the fleshy underbelly instead. The shark went for his abdomen as he yanked the spear out and went for the shark's neck again.

'*Air*,' Quinn's word rippled through the sea. '*She needs air.*'

The thought of his friend putting his mouth on her filled Thane with ugly jealousy. She belonged to him.

He jammed the spear into the shark's neck again and twisted it. In its last frenzied movement, the shark clamped its jaws onto Thane's waist and bit into his flesh before it died. Pain gripped him hard, but he pulled the precious spear out of the dead shark and made for the cavern. He reached them as Quinn made to put his mouth on Sara to give her breath. Thane wrenched her away from him and, through his haze of pain, fused his mouth to hers as they slipped through the dimension to the Golden City.

'*You're hurt,*' Quinn's words filtered through before Thane felt the blackness take him.

જાજા

She could finally see. Quinn had hold of Thane under his arms as they lost their sea forms. Blood oozed out of a wicked gash above Thane's hip.

"He's hurt," she screamed. "He needs help."

Quinn cried out in the language she couldn't understand. Males in white robes tied with gold sashes appeared instantly.

"The healers," Quinn said.

He said something else in his native language and a stern-faced male in a purple robe hurried toward her and made to take her away from Thane.

"No." She wrenched out of his grip. "Quinn, I want—I have—to be with him."

Quinn said something, took his spear from Thane, then left them. Purple robe muttered something then stared at her stomach. She followed the males in the white robes, who had hold of Thane, to a great hall filled with clear crystals. They put him on a marble table. His eyes were closed and he didn't speak. She stroked his head, trying to stay out of the way of the healers who surrounded him.

"I love you, Thane," she said.

"You may touch him," a female in a gold robe tied with a purple sash said in stilted English.

The males in white robes murmured among themselves. She put her palm on his smooth cheek. None of the males she'd seen in the Golden City sported beards or stubble. She'd never seen whiskers on Thane or Quinn when they were on land. She looked at Thane's magnificent, smooth, golden-skinned chest, then lower, avoiding the gash, to his scrotum and cock. She took a long breath. They were as she remembered them.

She realized she stood naked and inched closer to Thane in an effort to shield herself, although nobody seemed to notice her nudity.

"Sara."

Sara felt hands in her hair. Calista nodded toward two dark haired females in white robes. They held a white robe and sash in their hands. They came forward. Sara took her hands away from Thane. The women slipped her arms through the robe and tied it in the back then wrapped a purple sash around her waist.

"Thank you, tell them I said thank you," she said.

She stepped back to him. Still his eyes were closed. The males in white robes aimed light from large crystal wands across his body. They spoke to the female in the gold robe.

"Speak to him," Calista urged. "It will help him remember."

"Darling, please wake up. I have so many questions."

The women in white robes erupted in peals of giggles when she said "darling."

Calista spoke to them in soft tones and they left the chamber.

"They are my…" Calista seemed to search for a word. "…girls."

"Your daughters?" Sara said. Calista looked puzzled. "Yours."

Calista nodded.

"They are gorgeous," Sara said.

Calista looked puzzled again.

"They rock," Sara said. "Very pretty."

Calista smiled.

This would be hard, the language thing.

She sucked at languages in high school and college. Would she ever be fluent in Thane's native tongue?

She stroked his face while the woman in the gold robe aimed a green light at the gash in his abdomen.

Sara stepped away, but Calista shook her head. "You touch him, please. Send him love so he remembers."

Remembers? It was the second time she said that. Sara fought back the panicky tightness in her chest, put her palms on his shoulders, and covered his face with kisses.

"I love you, darling. I need you so much." She chanted the words over and over.

The men in white robes murmured words she didn't understand in a haunting melody.

Could he hear her voice or understand her words?

The woman in the gold robe passed a large crystal wand over Thane's torso then stepped back. The men in the white robes also stepped away. The woman gave what sounded like clipped instructions then left the healing chamber.

The men in white robes lingered, placing crystals around the room in various positions.

Thane murmured words in his native language and opened his eyes. She took her hands from his face and moved so he could see her.

"We made it, darling." She squeezed his hands and smiled through her tears.

He stared at her, puzzled, and said words in his language. His aunt touched his shoulder, and he smiled.

Sara shivered.

Thane's mother and Ronan came into the healing chamber. Bruna hung tightly to Ronan's arm as they approached Thane. Bruna touched her son's shoulder then pressed her cheek to his, murmuring softly. He answered his mother then shut his eyes again.

Bruna's face was a blank mask. "He doesn't remember your earth language or you," she said. "The trauma, he gave you breath when he was weak. We thank the life source he lives, no thanks to you." She glared at her.

"Bruna." Ronan spoke sharply.

"The love of my heart, then almost my son," Bruna hissed.

Sara couldn't breathe. "Quinn?" she whispered.

"He left," Bruna said.

Sara's throat closed up. She swayed. The men in white robes caught her before she hit the marble floor.

Chapter 8

Sara opened her eyes. She was spread out on a table, similar to the one Thane was put on, but on a much smaller room. The man in the purple robe waved a crystal wand over her body.

"No," she screamed. She sat up and shielded her belly. "No X-rays. They'll hurt the baby."

Nausea hit her then, and she swallowed hard. She felt fuzzy in her head.

"Sweet girl." Calista put her hand on her shoulder. "You are already such a good mum. The quartz does no harm. Your baby is good. You must take nourishment."

Calista held a crystal goblet to Sara's lips. It tasted like limeade, and she drank the whole goblet. Calista set a plate of shrimp, seaweed, and other morsels Sara didn't recognize in her lap. The man in the purple robe left them. She finished the entire plate, even the mystery food, which tasted fruity. Her head cleared and her nausea subsided, but her panic flared to life.

Thane didn't know her.

She was in a place where she was an alien, for all intents and purposes.

His mother hated her.

She didn't speak their language and only a handful of those who lived here spoke English, New Zealand style, but English, nonetheless.

She forced herself to take deep, steady breaths. She couldn't stop her tears.

She looked at Calista. "Thane?"

"He is good," Calista said. She brushed Sara's hair and Sara clutched her emerald necklace.

"Does he remember me?"

"Not yet"

"Will he? How long—what do the healers say?"

"Is not certain."

Bruna walked into the chamber—alone. Calista spoke rapidly in their native language. Bruna answered in short, clipped sentences.

Calista sighed then squeezed Sara's hands. "If Thane does not remember—"

Bruna interrupted. "You will not be acknowledged as his mate."

Sara's heart thundered in her chest. "What would I be?"

"An unchaste female with an unclaimed child," Bruna said.

"But our joining ceremony, we were in the Great Hall, everyone saw," Sara said.

"It doesn't matter. It's as if he has spurned you. It is like divorce on land," Calista said, weeping.

"But you may leave," Bruna said. "We are in the cusp of the solstice. You may slip back through the dimensions, but you must do so quickly, so the baby is safe."

Sara screamed in rage, her hand held protectively over her belly. "Don't you care about your grandchild? Don't you want to see him grow?"

"Yes," Bruna hissed. "Another I will grieve for till my life force leaves me. But unless Thane remembers, the baby will have no…" She struggled for a word.

"Others would say unkind things about you and the child."

Bruna stepped closer to them. She touched a strand of Sara's hair then stepped back "The healers say if he has not remembered yet—"

Sara squared her shoulders. She would not leave without a fight. She was her mother's daughter. "Where is he?"

"In the Great Hall taking nourishment," Bruna said.

Sara tugged on her necklace. "Let's go jog his memory."

Calista put her hand on her shoulder, halting her. "Jog?" She looked alarmed. "You must get your strength back before you run."

"Jog memory is figure of speech. It means make him remember."

"Oh." Calista said. She brushed Sara's hair then braided it so it hung over her shoulder. Then she rubbed lotion that smelled like sandalwood on her arms, hands, face, and then feet.

When she finished, Sara followed Bruna through a maze of granite corridors threaded with gold into the Great Hall, taking care to step around the channels of water.

Would she take sea form if she dipped her feet in the water?

Thane and the other males who sat at a log marble table stood when Bruna entered the Great Hall. He looked past Sara and smiled at his aunt.

All the breath left Sara's body, and she felt faint. Bruna nodded and all the males except Thane sat. Sara stepped closer to him. He looked her over but with no pleasure or flicker of recognition. Her heart hurt. She tugged on her necklace.

"Hi," she said.

He smiled. "You are new here." He remembered English. Her hope soared.

She stepped closer. Should she kiss him? Would he remember then?

"I'm Sara." She looked steadily into the green eyes she loved so much. "Your injury?"

"Is nothing," he said. "Just a shark."

"Do you remember the attack?"

"No." He rubbed his temples and drank from a goblet. "Bloody headache," he muttered.

Did his headache mean his memory was coming back?

Everyone in the Great Hall watched them. "I was with you when you were attacked. So was Quinn. You used his spear." She put her hand on his arm. "You saved my life."

"Thane?"

It was Dina. She sidled up to him and turned her face into his neck. Sara clenched her hands into fists. She looked at Bruna who stood silent. He shook Sara's hand off.

"Thane?" Sara felt faint and sank to her knees. He made no move to help her. "We are joined. You came on land, to Michigan, then Florida, to find me. I dreamed of you." She sobbed. "I carry your baby."

Thane shook his head. "You are human?"

"You saw her in the crystals and you would have no other," Calista said.

"Your mother does not approve," Sara said.

Dina inched closer to him and Sara wanted to do murder. She fought back a violent wav of nausea when he put his arm around Dina.

Tears streamed down her face. "Is Quinn here?" she sobbed.

Thane called for the healers. "It doesn't make sense, Sara." He looked at the healers. "Help her. She must go back to her kind." He turned away from her.

Sara stood up. "Damn you, Thane," she screamed, her panic and despair dissolving. "You will remember and it will be too late." She put her hands on his shoulders and fused her mouth to his then tore herself away. "The hell with you." She rounded on Bruna. "Fuck you, you bitter, hateful bitch. You'll never see your grandchild."

"She's fucked up," Dina said with a sneer, drawing closer to a bewildered-looking Thane.

'*In for a penny...*' Cinda's words never held so much meaning.

"You asshole," Sara said. "You saunter into my life, rip it apart, and then hang me out to dry. Cancer kicked my mother's ass, but you're not kicking mine. I was just fine without you. There's other fish in the sea." She laughed hysterically at her turn of phrase.

There was a commotion in the channel.

It was Quinn.

And Jumper.

She squealed with joy and jumped into the channel, her fear of water forgotten, to hug the dolphin. Jumper chortled in pleasure. Quinn's eyes narrowed in anger when he saw Thane's hand on Dina's waist.

"He's recovered but he doesn't remember me. I have to go back," she said.

"Asshole," Quinn said.

She laughed bitterly and nuzzled Jumper. "Goodbye, darling." She took a last look at the pink sky overhead.

Quinn took hold of her and lifted her out of the channel. Thane's eyes blazed with anger. Quinn hoisted himself out and took hold of her again.

She kissed his cheek. "Thank you, Quinn."

Quinn took hold of her chin. "I'll be back to check on you both." He touched Sara's flat stomach. She didn't see Thane put Dina away from him as Quinn pulled her out of the Great Hall through the maze of caverns, toward the chamber where she would slip through the dimensions to land.

༺༻

Searing pain blasted through Thane's head. Dina simpered something into his ear but he ignored her.

Why was his aunt weeping?

Why did Quinn's hands on the human woman fill him with rage? Quinn was his best mate.

She said he joined with her and she carried his seed, which the healers said was impossible. But he remembered the way she tasted when she kissed him and the way her skin smelled. His cock hardened instantly.

Bruna watched him steadily then closed her eyes and took a deep breath.

Damn his headache.

"Go after her, son and claim her," his mother said.

Calista smiled and nodded.

"Quinn, wait," Thane yelled.

He hurried to the chamber that transported those in the Golden City through the dimensions to land as fast as his throbbing head allowed. Jumbled images flooded his head—Sara holding onto a dolphin in the open sea, her screaming his name while he was buried in her sheath up to his balls.

"Sara, stop," he yelled. Pain throbbed through his head.

"Fuck off, asshole," she screamed. "I can't trust you. I'll never trust you. Send me back, Quinn."

Thane could see them in the distance. The quartz timepiece at the entrance to the chamber showed three minutes left in the earth solstice. His head pounded, and he lost his footing. Thane got to his feet and saw Quinn had Sara positioned in the chamber.

"Get her out of there, mate, please," Thane said. He moved toward them as fast as his throbbing temples allowed. There was only one minute left.

"Her choice, mate," Quinn said. "You fucked up."

Thane couldn't let her go. She belonged to him. He lunged toward her and clamped his hand around her ankle.

"Thank fuck," Quinn said.

Chapter 9

Sara tried to shake Thane off, but he squeezed her narrow ankle tighter as she pulled him through the dimensions. When they opened their eyes, they were sprawled on the floor of her apartment, still wearing the robes from the Golden City.

He let go of her ankle and rubbed it.

"I marked you, sorry, love. I couldn't let you go. My head was fucked up. You're my life. I remember now. Forgive me, love."

She looked at him warily. He stood then held out his hand to help her to her feet. She took it.

The pain in his head grabbed him again. "Bloody hell," he said.

"Sit down." She pointed to a chair. "I'll get you some ice," she said stiffly. She put a cold compress on the top of his head then sat across the room from him. "How and when will you go back?"

He noticed she didn't say "we."

"Love," he said.

"No," she screamed. "You don't get to call me that."

The pain in his head faded, and he moved so he was sitting next to her. He put the cold compress on her ankle he gripped so hard and held her foot in his lap.

"Does it hurt to walk on it, lo—"

"No. When will you leave?" Her lip trembled.

He trailed his hand up her thigh in a gentle caress. Her pupils dilated.

Thank fuck.

She wasn't immune to him.

"We, Sara, the question is when do we leave?"

Tears coursed down her cheeks. "I can't take the chance. It was something I'll never forget, but I have a child to raise. I have to give him the best chance I can."

"Him?"

She shrugged. "Just a feeling. Your healers didn't say. I can't go back," She looked at the floor. "I don't love you."

His head was clear and free of pain but a sick, cold feeling of dread settled in his chest. He took deep breaths to control it.

She loved him, he knew it.

But he had, for all intents and purposes, abandoned and spurned her in a place wholly alien to her. He had to play this right. It had to be her choice.

Her sea form, she loved her sea form.

He cradled her in his arms and lifted her off the couch. The compress fell to the floor.

My sweet little liar," he said against her ear.

She went stiff in his arms. "What are you doing?"

"A soak, for your ankle." He set her down, filled her tub, then undressed her and himself. He settled her in the tub against his back. He only touched her necklace. He knew she could feel his rock hard erection. She tried to squirm away from him, but he stroked her hip and she took her sea form.

She went limp against him, and he palmed her breasts in his hands. He tweaked her nipples, and she groaned. He needed the immersion but he did not take his sea form.

"How can you do this?" she said.

He bit her neck and pinched her nipple, and she went pliant in his arms.

"Do what, love?"

He noticed she didn't object when he called her "love."

"Stay the way you are when you make me like this."

He nipped her earlobe. "Make you like what, love?"

"Make me want you when I can't—"

"Can't what?"

"Join," she said.

"We are joined," he said, tugging on her necklace.

"Fuck, then. Is that what you want me to say, fuck, shag?"

He stroked her hip again, and her sea form left. He lifted her to face him then down until his cock was buried inside her.

⁂

"Is this what you want?" He lifted her as if she were a feather floating in the water and impaled her, hitting her G-spot.

Her words left. She could only moan.

"I fucked up, okay?" He plunged into her again. "My life force was weak. The last time you needed air—" He pressed his thumb onto her clit, and she squealed like Jumper. "The thought of Quinn putting his mouth on you—" He plunged again, hitting the back of her womb. "—made me insane. I used everything I had to get to you and lost my head." He pounded into her.

Intense spasms of pleasure rippled through her core and up her spine. He screamed her name and emptied himself inside her.

When she opened her eyes, she was cradled in his arms in her bed. He looked at her alarm clock.

Could she go back with him?

Why did he want her? She was so ordinary.

Dina was beautiful and obviously wanted him. And she had his mother's seal of approval.

Sara didn't realize she said the words out loud.

"Your spirit, your beautiful spirit, called to me through time and space, so I stole into your dreams. It was the only way I could have you. You fought so hard for your mother and carried on so bravely when she perished. I was determined never to join, not after what I saw my mother suffer when my father perished, until I found you." He nuzzled her neck. "I took you in your dreams to—"

She lifted her head to look at him. "Check me out? A quick shag? " She laughed.

"Yeah," he smirked. "And I was caught, love. Hopelessly. Forever. You are the most exquisite thing I've ever seen." He stood up and held out his hand to her. "Will you come with me, love, and let me love you and our babies under the pink sky until we draw our last breaths? And I should tell you we live a long time. Not like your land life spans."

"I love you, Thane, so much. Will you teach me the ways of the Golden City and sea forms? I guess I'm converting."

"Yes, love."

She smiled into his eyes, took his hand, and he pulled her through time and space until they stood together naked in the Great Hall amid shouts of joy. He fused his mouth to hers and she hung in his arms.

He let her go reluctantly.

"Do you join with Thane of your own free will?" a female in a purple robe asked in stilted English.

"Yes, I love him," she said.

Thane's eyes blazed with gold.

"It is done," the female said.

He lifted her in his arms and carried her through a maze of crystal hallways lined with gold.

"Our chambers, Sara." He set her down and took hold of her waist.

Crap. She forgot to ask. Did sea forms take more than one mate?

He shook his head. "No, love."

He read her thoughts. She'd forgotten he could do that.

"I'm yours as long as you draw breath." His eyes blazed with the golden lights she loved so much. "I have a surprise."

He led her to a room with a channel of water. There was a big splash and she saw Jumper. She and Jumper both squealed with joy. She jumped into the channel and hugged the dolphin. Jumper chortled with joy.

"Quinn went back for him," he said.

"I love him," she said. He looked murderous. "Not like I love you, darling."

He jumped into the channel and nuzzled her neck. "I love that," he said.

"What?"

"I love when you call me darling, much better than asshole."

She giggled.

"I remember when you said it when I was with the healers." He kissed her gently.

"We'll go back on land whenever we can to see your sire. But I'm not letting you out of my sight. Not sure if I'll be able to do that here."

"Your eco-missions." she said. "You must go."

"Can you live with that, love?"

She knew his father had perished that way. She knew that sea forms held the stewardship of the life forms and ecosystems under the waves sacred. She looked into the golden eyes she loved so much.

"Yes, darling. If I can come and help sometimes."

He pulled her into his arms while Jumper squealed in joy.

THE END

About the Author

Tara Eldana is the pen name of an award-winning staff writer for a weekly community newspaper chain in metro Detroit. She became hooked on romance fiction when her eleventh grade English teacher rejected the book report she wrote, saying the book was much too easy for her, and insisted she read and report on Daphne du Maurier's Rebecca. Eldana had read Margaret Mitchell's *Gone With the Wind* that previous summer.

She loves the romance genre and loves letting her characters take control of their stories. Eldana is a member of the Greater Detroit Romance Writers of America. Visit her at taraeldana.com, on Facebook, Instagram or Twitter. She loves to hear from her readers.

CPSIA information can be obtained
at www.ICGtesting.com
Printed in the USA
BVHW071503090719
552969BV00011B/205/P

9 781644 371633